DATE DUE

GAYLORD			PRINTED IN U.S.A.

43076
Summer Shepherd

Bonnie Highsmith Taylor
AR B.L.: 3.2
Points: 2.0   MG

Summer Shepherd

by Bonnie Highsmith Taylor

Perfection Learning®

Cover Illustration: Dea Marks
Inside Illustration: Dea Marks

For my husband Gene

Contents

1

Green Apples

It was the second time in a month that a policeman had come to the house.

The first time, I ran out the back door and hid in the alley. Mom was in her bedroom. She'd just gotten home from work. She didn't see me take off.

I stayed hidden until the policeman left our house. I watched him go across the street to the Hortons'.

Stan Horton had been with me when it happened. I didn't think it was such a big deal. The window hadn't broken.

It was actually Stan's green apple that had hit Old Man Jenks's window. I had thrown an apple too. But it only hit the side of Jenks's house. Besides, they were only tiny little apples.

We had gotten tired of Old Man Jenks. He had a fit just because we cut through his yard on the way home from school. We weren't hurting anything. It didn't hurt the fence to climb over it. And we didn't walk in his garden—no matter what he said.

I was sick of him calling us names. *Hoodlums* and *ruffians* were his favorites.

Mom didn't like him any better than I did. "But you know better than to act like that," she'd scolded. "No matter who it is. You don't throw things at him."

"I didn't throw anything at him," I said. "We waited till he went back in the house."

"You don't throw anything," she said. "And you know it."

"But he called us names. I was so mad. I guess I wasn't thinking straight."

The second time the police came, it was a lot more serious than throwing green apples at Old Man Jenks's house.

It was for stealing. It was the first time I'd ever stolen anything. And I got caught.

Stan and I wanted to go to the picture show. We didn't have any money. Mom said to wait till payday. Then I could go.

But Saturday was the last night the show was playing. It was two swell adventure movies.

Friday night, Stan said, "I know how we can get some money for the show."

"How?" I wanted to know.

"We can . . ." Stan paused. He acted embarrassed. "Well . . . we can trade in some milk bottles."

"I don't think Mom will give me any," I said. "She has to put them out for the milkman."

"I mean . . . well, you know," Stan went on. "We can get some off porches. After dark."

"Are you crazy?" I exclaimed. "That's stealing!"

"Just a couple apiece. Enough for the show."

Bottles were worth a nickel each. It cost a dime to get into the show. Until you were 12. Then it cost a quarter.

I wouldn't be 12 for three more weeks. My birthday was in June.

I didn't say anything. I just stared at Stan.

"A dime, for Pete's sake," Stan said. "It's not like we're robbing a bank."

"It's still stealing," I replied. "And what if we get caught?"

"We won't. Trust me."

Like a dope, I trusted him.

Because of the war, people couldn't turn on porch lights. And they kept their blinds closed tightly. The darkness protected them in case of an invasion. Stan explained that it made stealing the bottles easier.

We waited until after dark on Friday. Then we sneaked out. Mom had company. A couple of women from the shipyard where she worked had come over. They were playing cards and listening to *Henry Aldrich* on the radio. Mom didn't pay any attention when I went out.

Stan and I walked about four blocks from where we lived. "We don't want to take them from anyone we know," he said.

I argued with him a little as we walked. "Why not wait till next Saturday?" I said. "I think Mom might give me a little allowance on payday. There might be a good show on then too."

"Not as good as an Errol Flynn movie. And the other one is a Western," he argued. "Besides, you never get to spend your allowance on what you want."

He was right—in a way. I only got an allowance when Mom could afford it. That wasn't very often. And usually I spent most of it on defense saving stamps.

Mom didn't make me buy saving stamps. But she kept reminding me that a lot of things were important. Because of the war.

We did all the things we were supposed to do. Mom saved all of her bacon grease and turned it in. You got two ration stamps for a pound of used grease.

We also saved our tin cans. And I collected old newspapers all over the neighborhood and turned them in.

Stan collected newspapers too. But he sold them and used the money on stuff for himself.

We planted a victory garden in our backyard. We grew our own vegetables to eat. That way, the things the farmers grew could feed the men in the service.

Mom didn't drive our car. It was on blocks in the garage. Dad put it there before he went in the army.

"When I get home," he'd said, "we'll go for rides every day. Twice on Sundays."

But Dad wasn't coming home. Not ever. Because Dad was dead.

2

Milk Bottles

Stealing the bottles was awful. My heart was beating so hard, it hurt. Stan grabbed two bottles off one porch. I grabbed two off the porch across from it. Then I ran. I ran so fast that Stan could hardly keep up.

We collapsed in his backyard. When we finally got our breath back, we stashed the bottles in his woodshed.

"We'll take them down to Fred's Market in the morning," said Stan. "You wait about an hour after I go in. Then you take yours in."

The store was almost empty when I walked in. I waited for an hour after Stan. I carried a bottle in each arm.

Fred was waiting on Mrs. Sands. I knew it would take him a while. Mrs. Sands liked to talk. And Fred was a good listener. He was always really friendly.

Fred delivered groceries for people. Some customers had to walk a long way. Others had too much to carry.

He delivered for Mom and me a lot. Mom always gave him a cup of coffee. Fred always said she made the best coffee he'd ever tasted.

"For war coffee," he'd laugh.

Now Mrs. Sands was saying, "Did I tell you that Billy made first class?"

"That's good," Fred said. "As smart as he is, he'll be a general in no time."

Mrs. Sands smiled. "I don't know about that. I just wish I had him home. I wish all our boys were home."

"I wish so too, Mrs. Sands," Fred said. "I wish this lousy war was over. And the world was back to normal."

Billy was Mrs. Sands' son. He was in the army, overseas someplace. He was only 19.

Fred had a younger brother who was in the navy. "I haven't heard from Mickey for over a month now," he said. "And that's not like him. He usually writes every week."

It made me remember the letters we got from Dad. Mom and I looked forward to them so much. We still had all of them.

Sometimes I'd take them out of the desk drawer and read them. A lot of them had things blacked out. Censored.

The military didn't want soldiers sending important war information to their family and friends. So the letters that the soldiers wrote were read before they were sent. And our letters to them were read too.

I set my bottles down at the end of the counter. Fred finished with Mrs. Sands. She had been doing some shopping while she visited with Fred.

Fred smiled at me.

Mrs. Sands smiled too and said, "Hello, Jackie."

She never stopped calling me *Jackie*. It started when I was really little. She took care of me once in a while when Mom and Dad went out. She made cookies for Billy and me.

Billy was a lot older than I was. But he'd play with me anyway. Once he even let me help him make a model plane.

I hoped nothing happened to him. He was a nice guy. And he was Mrs. Sands' only kid.

Mrs. Sands took her ration books out of her purse. She took out the stamps she needed for her groceries.

"Six points for cheese," she complained. "But I do love my cheese. Maybe I should take a pound of bacon. It's eight points a pound. But it goes a long way. I don't buy much meat with Billy gone."

Mrs. Sands stopped suddenly. "Here I am, complaining about having to go without a few things," she said. "And our boys are over there dying on battlefields and—"

I saw the look Fred gave her.

She put her groceries in her shopping bag. Then she said, "You say 'hello' to your mama, Jackie."

"I will," I answered.

After she left, Fred picked up the bottles. He put them in a wooden box with some other milk bottles.

"Two quarts of milk, Jack?" asked Fred. "Your mother doing some baking?"

I gulped. "Uh . . . no. I just wanted to trade them in."

"You want to buy candy?" Fred asked.

"No," I mumbled.

Fred handed me a dime. I put it in my pocket and started to leave.

"How about a jawbreaker?" Fred asked. He reached into a big round glass bowl on the counter. I took the jawbreaker he handed me. I mumbled "thanks" and left.

Outside, I put the jawbreaker in my mouth. I sucked on it. But it didn't taste right. It left a bad taste in my mouth.

I knew it wasn't the jawbreaker. It was my guilt. I spit the jawbreaker out in the gutter and ran down the street.

I told Mom that Stan had loaned me the money for the show. Stan told his mother that I had loaned him the money. Great, I thought. I not only stole for the first time. But I told Mom a lie as well.

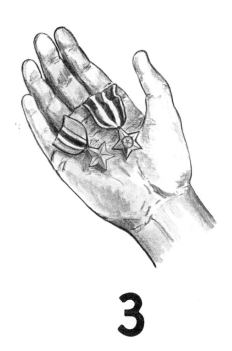

3

Silver and Bronze Stars

It was Sunday morning when the policeman came.

The look on Mom's face was almost as bad as the day we got the news about Dad. That was the worst day of my life. The Sunday morning the police came was the next worst day.

It would be a cinch. That's what Stan had told me. What I didn't know was that Stan had done it before. In fact, he'd done it lots of times. That's why Fred got suspicious.

One of the women whose bottles we had stolen came into the store the next morning. She told Fred what had happened. Fred called the police.

So now I was standing there wishing I was dead. The policeman asked me a lot of questions. I'm not even sure what I said.

After the policeman left, Mom just sort of collapsed in a chair.

I couldn't even move for a long time. I just stood there waiting. Even though I was chilled, I could feel the sweat pouring out of me.

It seemed like hours before Mom finally said anything. It didn't even sound like her voice. "I can't believe you'd do something like that, Jack. Why?"

She was looking at me. And there were tears in her eyes.

I'd never made my mom cry before. Never. I tried to answer. But there was nothing I could say.

What could I say? That I wanted to go to the show and I didn't have the money? That it was no big deal? It was only two milk bottles? Only ten cents?

That's what Stan would say. But I knew it was a big deal—a really big deal. I knew by the miserable feeling in the pit of my stomach.

I'd even felt awful in the theater. I didn't enjoy the movie at all. But I didn't want Stan to know. So I pretended I was having a great time.

Mom asked me again, "Why, Jack?"

I swallowed hard and shrugged my shoulders. I really wanted to cry. But I wouldn't in front of her.

Then Mom said, "What would your dad say, Jack? If he were here."

That did it! The dam inside me broke loose.

"He's not here!" I screamed. "He's not here and he never will be! He's dead! He's dead!"

I ran out of the room. When I got to my bedroom, I threw myself down on the bed. I squeezed my eyes shut as tightly as I could. I squeezed until I saw colored spots in the dark. Then I pulled the pillow over my head and let loose.

I'm sure Mom must have heard me. But she didn't come in. Maybe because she was crying too.

Stan and I had to go to a hearing and talk to a judge.

Mom and I rode with Mrs. Horton. Stan's dad was working in Alaska. He only came home about once a month.

Stan had two sisters. But they were a lot older. And both were married.

I couldn't believe it. Mrs. Horton didn't act like she was mad at Stan. She didn't seem hurt or anything.

17

She was just upset because she had to use the last of her gasoline ration to drive downtown. Mom gave her some money to pay for taking us.

It had been nearly a week since the policeman had come to the house. Mom hadn't mentioned it once. I wondered why. But I didn't ask. I didn't want to talk about it.

But I'd been scared to death the whole time. Not knowing what was going to happen was scary. I knew Stan was as scared as I was. But he tried not to show it.

It turned out that it wasn't as bad as I thought it was going to be. The judge was really nice. I was more embarrassed and ashamed than anything. And he made me feel even worse.

The judge said things like, "You should be thinking about the horrible things that are going on all over the world right now. Instead of doing things to cause unhappiness for your parents."

He looked right at me when he said, "You've never been in trouble before. Do you want some foolish thing you did as a child to follow you all of your life?"

I mumbled, "No, sir."

Stan mumbled, "No, sir."

The judge asked me about school. I told him I liked it okay. I got pretty good grades in most subjects.

He lectured Stan a little. He seemed to realize that it had been Stan's idea.

Then he said, "I have a feeling I'll never see you boys in my courtroom again. Am I right?"

We both said, "Yes, sir."

When we got into the backseat and started home, I waited for Stan to make some wisecrack. But he didn't.

Finally I said, "The judge was okay, wasn't he?"

Stan answered, "Yeah, he was pretty nice."

Mom used one of our meat ration stamps to buy a round steak for dinner. She simmered it for hours and hours. It was still a little tough. But it tasted great. We were lucky to get any meat at all.

Some of the butcher shops were selling horse meat. But Mom had never bought any.

"I just know I couldn't eat it," she'd said.

I was glad. Every time I thought about eating horse meat, I pictured Roy Rogers' horse Trigger in my mind.

I felt bad about Mom missing work on account of me. But she didn't say anything.

I hated that Mom had to work in the shipyard. I knew it was really hard work. She came home so tired. Sometimes she could hardly move.

I helped around the house as much as I could. I wasn't much good at cooking. But I tried. Mom said my bread pudding was better than hers. But I thought she just said that to make me feel good.

Bread pudding was one of our favorite things. But it took a lot of sugar. And sugar was rationed. So I didn't make it often.

I could also make scrambled eggs and French toast. But my oatmeal was a joke with us. Mom said I could make a fortune selling the lumps for golf balls.

Before Dad had joined the army, Mom never worked anyplace—except at home. I knew she was worried about what was going to happen after the war was over. The men would come home and take back all the jobs. Mom said there might not even be any shipyards then.

That night, I finally apologized to Mom. It was hard to do. All I said was, "I'm really sorry, Mom. About what I did."

She just said, "I know you are, Jack."

Then she gave me a hug, and I went to bed.

But I didn't go to sleep—not for a long time. I opened the box on my dresser and took out Dad's medals. The army had sent them to Mom.

There was a Silver Star and a Bronze Star. They sent a certificate of bravery too. Because Dad died a hero. He was killed saving some other guys' lives.

The certificate was in a frame hanging on the living room wall. But Mom let me keep the medals in my room.

I lay down on my bed. I held the Silver Star in one hand and the Bronze Star in the other. I did this a lot. Sometimes I cried. And sometimes I didn't.

I opened my hands and looked at the medals. They were all I had left of my dad—besides some really great memories.

I felt sad sometimes. They were my dad's medals. But he had never even seen them.

4

Charlie

School would be out in a couple of weeks. I could hardly wait. School wasn't too bad. But I was looking forward to summer vacation.

I was going to eastern Oregon to spend the summer on my uncle's sheep ranch. Actually, I wouldn't be spending the summer *on* the ranch. I would be going to the mountains with his herder to tend the sheep.

Uncle Brad said that his herder, Charlie Hayes, was getting up in years. He didn't want him to be out all alone.

It was also hard to find help these days. Almost everyone was in the service or working in the shipyards. So Uncle Brad was grateful that I could help out for the summer.

Mom hoped that being at the ranch would keep me out of trouble. I hadn't stepped out of line once since the milk-bottle incident. But I knew Mom still worried about me.

She also thought I needed some "male influence." With Dad gone, she thought that spending time with Uncle Brad and Charlie Hayes would be good for me.

I was excited about going. I couldn't believe how much Uncle Brad was going to pay me. I'd be able to buy all of my school clothes. And I hoped I would have enough to buy a good used bike.

But I was kind of nervous too. I'd never been away from home for more than a week. That had been when I was ten. I went to church camp. I remembered how homesick I got.

And I didn't know Uncle Brad and his family very well. Uncle Brad was Dad's older brother. He and Aunt Margie had a little girl, Lois. She was ten.

I also wondered what Charlie would be like. I'd be spending most of my time with him. Hopefully, we'd get along.

The night before I left, Mom and I went to the picture show. They were both good movies. But one was a war picture, and I knew it made Mom sad. It made me a little sad too. After the show, we stopped at the drugstore and had lemon Cokes.

I packed my stuff that night before I went to bed. Uncle Brad had said to wear old clothes and good sturdy shoes.

I only had one pair of shoes that fit me. Shoes were rationed. It would probably be fall before I could get some new ones for school.

I got on the bus in downtown Portland. It was a little after eight o'clock in the morning. I had a little bit of a lump in my throat when I waved good-bye to Mom.

Then the next thing I knew, we were on our way. After about two hours, I fell asleep.

It was a long ride to Hayville. My legs were shaking a little when I got off the bus. I was pretty nervous about seeing Uncle Brad and the rest of the family.

But Uncle Brad was the only one who had come to get me. He had an old blue pickup. It was parked at the curb across the street from the bus station. He grinned and shook hands with me.

"You're the spitting image of Johnny when he was your age," he said.

It took me a minute to realize he was talking about Dad. No one that I knew had ever called him Johnny. He was always John. And I was Jack, short for John Owen Baker, Junior.

It was a long drive to Uncle Brad's ranch. And it was the bumpiest road I'd ever been on.

Aunt Margie and my cousin Lois were waiting for us. They were sitting on the big front porch.

I couldn't believe the size of the house. Nine rooms, I found out later. The living room, dining room, kitchen, and one bedroom were downstairs. There was also a room that served as a library and Uncle Brad's office. Upstairs, there were four more bedrooms.

Plus, there was a bathroom upstairs *and* one downstairs. I figured they must be rich.

I couldn't see outside very well. It was too dark. But the silence was unbelievable. It was never this quiet back home.

Aunt Margie made me a sandwich. It was so thick. I could hardly get it into my mouth. Then she gave me a big piece of chocolate cake. It was delicious. I drank two glasses of cold milk. I was starved—and dead tired.

Then Aunt Margie said, "Now this boy needs to go to bed before he drops." I didn't argue.

My room was nice. It had a double bed. I'd never slept in a double bed before. It was weird.

I felt like I'd been away from home for months. I was already homesick. I thought about Mom. I wondered if she was lying in bed thinking about me.

As sleepy and tired as I was, I couldn't fall asleep right away. What was it going to be like? I wondered. Would I be sorry I came?

It was totally silent. Then, all of a sudden, there was a sound. It was frogs croaking. There must have been hundreds of them.

Then I heard another sound. I decided it had to be an owl. It sounded pretty close too. It was probably in one of those big, tall trees I'd seen when we pulled into the driveway.

I closed my eyes and lay there listening. They were great sounds to fall asleep to. They didn't seem to disturb the silence.

But the next sound I heard did. It was the first time I'd ever heard a rooster crow.

How could it possibly be morning already? It seemed like I had just fallen asleep. But now there were dogs barking and doors slamming. And from somewhere, a motor was starting.

I sat up in bed and looked out the window. It wasn't quite light yet. The motor sound I'd heard was a tractor. I couldn't see the person driving it very well. But I knew it wasn't Uncle Brad.

I got up and pulled on my clothes. I went downstairs.

Aunt Margie was putting breakfast on the table. Boy, what a breakfast! You'd never have known there was a war going on. We had sausage and eggs and pancakes with thick, creamy butter.

"The only rationing that bothers us much is on gas," said Uncle Brad. "We have to be a little careful."

"And sugar," added Aunt Margie. "I never have enough sugar for canning and baking anymore."

"After we eat, I'll take you out to meet Charlie," said Uncle Brad.

It didn't take me long to put away that great breakfast. My cousin Lois chattered all the time I was eating. I thought she was pretty nice and friendly. She told me all about a calf she was raising for 4-H.

Uncle Brad got his hat off the wall hook. I heard him whisper to Aunt Margie, "I'm not looking forward to springing this on Charlie."

Springing it on Charlie? I wondered what that meant.

I followed Uncle Brad. We passed a big orchard and a pond. We came to a building in a grove of trees.

Uncle Brad said, "This is where the help bunks. Right now there's only Charlie and Red. Red works around here doing odd jobs."

I figured he must be who I had seen driving the tractor.

"We'll be haying soon," Uncle Brad went on. "Then the bunkhouse will be full. The help will stay on till all the fruit is harvested too."

He stopped just before we reached the building. "Now, Jack," he said. "Don't worry about Charlie. He does a lot of barking. But his bite's not so bad."

We went into the bunkhouse. Charlie was sitting at a table that was nailed to the wall. He was just finishing a plate of fried potatoes and ham.

"Hi, Charlie," said Uncle Brad. "I'd like you to meet my nephew Jack. He's from Portland. He's going to spend the summer."

Charlie stood up. He wasn't very tall, and he humped over just a little. "Jack, this is Charlie Hayes," said Uncle Brad.

Charlie didn't exactly smile. But he put out his hand. It was rough.

Then Uncle Brad explained that I was going to be his helper with the herd.

I thought the old man was going to explode. "Helper! Helper! He's hardly out of diapers! If you think I'm going to play nursemaid to a young whelp, you've got another think coming!"

I could feel my face getting hot. I was so embarrassed. But I was mad too. He sounded just like Old Man Jenks.

What the heck was I doing here? I thought. I should have known there'd be a catch. The old man didn't want any part of me. And I didn't want any part of him.

"Listen, Charlie," Uncle Brad tried to explain. "You know how bad your rheumatism is getting. He can help with some of the lifting and—"

"I don't have rheumatism! And there isn't any lifting. And you know it! As for the sheep, the dogs do most of the work. And you know that too."

I couldn't believe he could talk that way to Uncle Brad. Uncle Brad was his boss, after all.

Uncle Brad motioned for me to go outside. I did—gladly. I sure wished I was back home. I had no desire to spend the summer with that old man. No matter how much I got paid.

5

"Boy"

But two days later, we were on our way.

We loaded the herder's wagon the night before. The wagon was like a little house on wheels. It had a built-in bunk bed. And there was a small stove with a stove pipe that went through the roof. There were also lots of cupboards.

Charlie had said there wasn't any lifting. But I carried a lot of heavy things into the wagon.

First I hauled an iron pot he called a *Dutch oven*. Then I loaded a kerosene camp stove. There were lots of groceries too, including a 50-pound sack of potatoes. The sleeping bags were the lightest things I tossed into the wagon.

We filled a big barrel on the back of the wagon with water. But Uncle Brad said we'd be grazing near rivers and streams most of the time.

The night before we left, I wrote Mom a letter. I decided not to tell her about how Charlie had acted. It would just upset her.

So I told her how nice Uncle Brad and Aunt Margie were. And I told her how great it was at night going to sleep to the sound of the frogs and the owl.

Just before I climbed up on the seat next to Charlie, Uncle Brad whispered, "It'll be better in a day or two. Charlie's okay. He'll cool off."

To both of us, he said, "I'll be bringing fresh supplies in about two weeks or so."

We hadn't even gotten out of the farmyard before I made a fool of myself. "What's the horse's name, Mr. Hayes?" I asked.

He looked at me, disgusted. "Her name's Kate. And she isn't a horse. She's a mule."

The dogs were Buster and Rosie. I couldn't believe how smart they were. And the way they kept the sheep together was amazing. If even one sheep got out of line, a dog would turn it back. Sometimes, if a dog had to get to the other side of the herd, it would walk right on top of the sheep.

Charlie could whistle or make a signal with his hand, and the dogs would do just what he wanted them to. I liked the dogs a lot. They were good company.

And so far, I liked the sheep. They were woolly and warm. And they didn't look very dangerous.

Now if I could just learn to like Charlie Hayes.

Noon came. Charlie hadn't said another word to me yet.

I just sat there, bouncing on the seat next to him. It was really uncomfortable. Not just from the bouncing, but from the way he was acting.

Then finally, he said, "We'll eat here."

We ate ham sandwiches that Aunt Margie had fixed. She had also packed cookies and apples.

Charlie gave the dogs water from the barrel. I reached down and petted them while they drank. They panted and slurped my hand with their wet tongues.

Then they bounded away. They went back to their job of taking care of the sheep.

I felt funny sitting there eating in silence. I tried to think of something to say. I could hear both of us chewing—even over the baaing of the sheep.

At last, I said, "The dogs sure are smart, aren't they, Mr. Hayes?"

All he said was, "Yep."

We finished eating and moved on. We started climbing some. There were a few trees here and there. Some of them were growing in bunches of ten to twenty. They had light-colored bark and little round green leaves. I wanted to know what they were. But I was afraid I'd say something dumb if I asked.

I hoped Uncle Brad was right about things getting better in a couple of days.

Just about the time the sun sank behind the hills, we came to a beautiful meadow. It was green and pretty. And did it ever smell good!

There were tall pine and fir trees. I also spotted more of the leafy trees we had seen before. But I still didn't have the courage to ask Charlie their name.

The sheep headed for the creek immediately. They drank for a while. Then they started nibbling the green grass.

The dogs flopped down on the ground to rest. But they never took their eyes off the sheep. Once in a while, a lamb would get separated from its mother and really bellow. But the mother would find it right away.

"Boy," said Charlie. "Make a campfire. Not too big."

Whew! At least that was something I knew how to do. I'd built lots of campfires when we went camping on the beach. We'd also learned how to build them at church camp.

In no time, I had a fire going. I'd also gathered a stack of wood from under the trees.

Charlie fed some oats to Kate. Then he ran a long rope between two trees and tied her to it.

"Boy," the old man said again. "See this." He held out what looked like a long cane. "It's a shepherd's crook. Lots of herders don't use them. But they come in handy sometimes. You can slow down a sheep by hooking that curved end around a leg."

I remembered seeing Bible pictures of shepherds holding them. I never knew what they were used for.

I also wondered if Charlie Hayes was going to call me "boy" all summer.

At dusk, we ate dinner. I learned one good thing about Charlie. He was a terrific cook.

We had fried potatoes and onions with chopped-up bacon in it. And he made biscuits in that Dutch oven.

He gave me a cup of coffee. It was bitter. But I didn't want to hurt his feelings or make him mad. So I drank it. I wondered what Mom would have said if she knew I was drinking coffee.

After dinner, Charlie took out a pipe and lit it.

When it started to get dark, I saw that the sheep had bedded down. Most of them were asleep. Every once in a while, the dogs would make a circle around them. Then they'd lie back down.

I helped wash the dishes. Charlie dumped out the coffee grounds and filled the pot with water.

It was dark when we went to bed. We crawled inside the wagon. I put my sleeping bag on the floor at one end. Charlie slept in his bunk at the other end.

I made myself comfortable. Suddenly, I heard a long, low howl. I sat up in bed.

"Just a coyote," Charlie said in the dark. "It's a long way off."

I heard a dog growl.

"Will they . . . will they hurt the sheep?" I asked. I knew that coyotes killed sheep.

"They'll try to," said the old man. "It's our job to see that they don't."

The coyote howled again. Then another one. This one was a little closer. I felt a chill run through me. Goose bumps covered my arms. I didn't like that sound one bit.

After a while, the howling died down. Finally, I drifted off to sleep.

Morning came early. We had bacon and some of the biscuits from the night before. Charlie put a handful of coffee into the pot and boiled it. It was still bitter. But at least it was hot. It was a nippy morning.

"What do you want me to do, Mr. Hayes?" I asked Charlie.

"You can feed the dogs. Break up those leftover biscuits and pour the bacon grease on them."

Boy, did they ever gulp that down. The dogs slurped me in the face. It made me laugh. Then they hurried back to the sheep.

Charlie walked around the herd. Every once in a while, he'd grab a hold of a sheep with the crook. He'd look it over and then set it free. Later I learned that he was checking for burrs or sores that might be hidden in the sheep's wool.

I could tell one thing about Charlie. He liked animals and they liked him.

Kate nuzzled his neck when he rubbed her head. Both dogs tried to be the first one to be petted when he came near. I think even the sheep liked him. I noticed he spent a lot of time watching the lambs play. Once or twice, I even saw him grin a little.

6

Seeking Peace

I sure wished Charlie was a little more talkative. I wasn't used to being around people like him. I didn't know if it was because he didn't like me or what.

Uncle Brad hadn't told me a thing about him. But I figured if Charlie spent every summer herding sheep all alone, it might be that he didn't care much for people.

Some days, Charlie's silence just about drove me crazy. And I was awfully homesick.

I'd go off by myself a lot. But I made sure to keep an eye on the herd.

I spent more and more time thinking about Dad. I missed him more than ever. We'd had some really good times together.

One day I walked along the creek alone. I could still see the camp and the sheep. Charlie was sitting by the fire smoking his pipe.

I lay down on my stomach. I lay very still. Soon some minnows started swimming around in the water. I watched them, hardly breathing.

I grinned when I thought about the first time Dad took me fishing.

Every two minutes, Dad had said, "Now you be careful, Jack. Don't stand up in the boat. You might fall in."

I knew I might fall in. I wasn't about to stand up in the boat. I could see how deep the water was. And I sure didn't want to fall in it.

So I sat still like Dad told me. And I held my pole like he told me. And I didn't fall in.

But Dad did.

We were close to a tree that had limbs hanging out over the water. Dad's line got tangled in a limb when he cast out. He reached out to untangle it. But he reached too far. He fell into the water with a big splash.

It scared me. I thought for sure he was going to drown. I didn't know how to save him. And I didn't know how to get back to shore alone.

But Dad got out okay. He didn't say a word. He rowed to shore and turned the rented boat in.

Then we got in the car and went home. Dad didn't say a word all the way home. Neither did I.

Dad didn't laugh. I didn't laugh. But Mom just about died laughing when she saw Dad. His clothes were still so wet he could hardly walk.

After he changed his clothes, Mom asked, "How many fish did you catch?"

Then she broke down laughing again.

I couldn't see what was so funny then. But when I got a little older, I thought it was hilarious. Dad thought so too.

It was just one of the things Mom liked to tease Dad about. Mom always had a swell sense of humor—even better than Dad. She could always see the funny side of everything. Until Dad died.

Now it was like we were different people. Both of us realized that we had to go on without Dad. But neither of us really knew how.

I was very intent on watching the minnows. I let my mind wander back to the past.

Then something cold and wet touched the back of my neck. I must have jumped about a foot. It's a wonder I didn't fall in the creek.

When I flipped over, I was looking into Rosie's face.

"Rosie girl!" I cried. "You just about scared me to death."

She whined and licked me all over. Her tongue lapped my arms and neck and face. I put my arms around her and hugged her hard. I buried my face in her soft fur.

"Good girl, Rosie," I murmured again and again.

She let me hold her and pat her for a while. Then she broke loose and ran back to the herd.

I was sure glad the animals were friendly. Even Kate liked me. And I was a little bit afraid of her.

I wandered around the meadow for a while. It was so beautiful there. The mountains, the trees, and the wildflowers surrounded me.

I began to notice the birds. I hadn't known there were so many different kinds of birds. I really liked the meadowlarks. They had the best song.

One was perched on a bush not far away. It threw back its head and started singing. I tried to imitate it. But I didn't even come close.

All I did was confuse Buster and Rosie. They started circling the herd, barking and nipping at the sheep. The poor sheep almost went crazy. I guess they were trying to figure out what they'd done wrong. They'd been grazing quietly, doing just what sheep were supposed to do.

I couldn't keep from giggling a little. It was pretty funny. But if Charlie was watching, would he think it was funny?

I decided to give up whistling.

I picked a bunch of wildflowers and headed back to the camp.

Charlie was sewing up a tear in the leg of his pants. He was grumbling to himself.

When he saw the flowers, he said, "Mighty pretty. There are some fruit jars in the cupboard. You can put them in one."

The flowers looked really nice on the little wooden stand in the wagon.

7

A Visitor

One day Charlie was having a little trouble getting around. He was limping pretty bad.

I was sure it was from his rheumatism. But I wouldn't say so for anything. Not when he'd told me he'd twisted his ankle a little when he slipped and fell.

"It happened when I was pulling burrs out of a lamb," he'd said. "The little fellow got scared. He jumped around and . . . and tripped me."

But I had seen him limping when he first got up that morning. He'd even had a little trouble getting down the wagon step. And he hadn't even checked on the sheep yet.

I asked, "Do you want me to rub your ankle? Or put some hot packs on it?"

Charlie just shook his head.

"You better sit around camp until it gets better," I said. "I'll take care of things."

And I did. I fixed a late breakfast. It was only some bacon (which I burned) and a can of pears. But it was breakfast.

Charlie even drank my coffee without saying anything. And I knew it wasn't as strong as he liked it.

I did up the dishes and fed Rosie and Buster. They kept jumping on Charlie and licking him in the face.

"They act like they know there's something wrong with you," I said.

"Animals are smart," he answered.

They were sure great dogs. I threw a stick for them. I watched them tussle over it. They only played for a little while. Then they were back to their job of herding the sheep.

A Visitor

I circled the sheep and looked them over. I pulled burrs and dry sticks out of the wool of a couple of sheep. I discovered one older ewe with a cut on her foot. I went back to the wagon and got the tarry stuff that Charlie used for cuts and sores.

Charlie was sitting on the ground, leaning against the wagon wheel. He was sound asleep. He didn't even hear me go in and out of the wagon. The way he was snoring, he couldn't have heard anything.

A couple of chipmunks were nibbling on a canned pear. I'd dropped it on the ground at breakfast. They sure looked funny with pear juice all over their faces.

A blue jay was scolding them from a pine-tree limb. I guess he wanted some too.

I took care of the ewe with the injured foot. I checked over some of the other sheep. The herd seemed to be okay.

I wandered into a wooded area. It was so pretty in the mountains. I thought I could live there forever.

I sat down on a fallen log. I could still see the herd from where I was.

The sun streamed through the trees. It felt good as it shone on my back. I could have fallen asleep.

I sat there looking at the trees. There was a small open area. A couple of willow trees grew there. The grass was tall and green.

After a few moments, I saw a movement in the grass. I watched closely. It was a little gray rabbit. It was nibbling away at a blade of grass. The grass was sideways in its mouth. Its pink nose twitched.

Then suddenly, I saw another movement. I froze even more. My heart started thumping when I saw what the movement was. A bobcat crept from behind a stump.

I had never seen a bobcat in my life—except in books and movies. It was huge. And it was beautiful.

The bobcat inched slowly toward the rabbit. It was about ten feet away when the rabbit spotted it. I didn't know anything could move as fast as that rabbit did. The bobcat tore behind it. Clods of dirt flew up from the ground.

The bobcat sprang through the air. One paw came down on the rabbit. The rabbit gave a pitiful squeal. I closed my eyes quickly. I didn't want to see it.

But when I opened them, the rabbit was gone. The bobcat was disappearing into the woods. He had missed this time.

I was happy for the rabbit. But I was sad for the bobcat who had missed his breakfast.

I stood up and started back to the camp. I could hardly wait to tell Charlie what I'd seen.

As I reached the camp, a man on a horse rode in. Charlie got to his feet.

"Howdy, Red," he greeted the man. "What's going on? Where's Mr. Baker?"

The redheaded man got off his horse. He stretched and walked around a little. I saw that he was lame. One leg was a little shorter than the other.

He was young—maybe in his twenties. And he had the reddest hair and about a million red freckles.

I had seen him a couple of times at the ranch. But I'd never met him. He grinned and said "hi" to me.

"Mr. and Mrs. Baker had to go to Farwell," Red explained. "Mrs. Baker's mother had to have an operation. Nothing serious. But they'll be gone a day or two."

Red hadn't been able to bring many supplies on his horse. But he did bring me a letter from Mom. She didn't say a whole lot. Just that she'd gotten my letter and she missed me. She also mentioned that Fred said "hi." I thought that was kind of strange.

It was great having Red in camp. He was a real talker. And he kept me laughing the whole time he was there.

He and Charlie were both interested when I told them about the bobcat.

"I'll stay the night," Red said. "But they need me back at the ranch soon. The haying crew is there. And they're getting ready to harvest some of the fruit too."

Charlie cooked a good dinner that night. Red had brought some eggs. They were in a little sack of cornmeal so they wouldn't break. We had fried potatoes and eggs and coffee. It was so good.

Red had also brought some ripe, juicy plums. They would be a treat.

After dinner, Charlie said, "You bring that mouth organ with you, Red?"

"Sure did," Red grinned.

He took a harmonica out of his shirt pocket. Could he ever play that harmonica! He played a lot of songs that I knew.

When he started playing "Down in the Valley," Buster and Rosie started howling. They howled and howled along with the music.

Then, way off, there was another howl.

Charlie laughed. "Guess that coyote doesn't like your music any better than the dogs."

A Visitor

It was a really great night. We sat around the campfire—talking, laughing, and listening to the music.

I slept outside on the ground with Red that night. I lay awake for a long time. Looking up at the sky, I saw millions and millions of stars.

I missed Mom a lot. But I sure loved being there.

I wished that Red didn't have to go back in the morning. But he rode off before daylight.

8

Lessons

At the end of a couple of weeks, I had learned a lot about sheep. First of all, sheep are stupid. Charlie said if one sheep jumped over a cliff, the rest of them would follow. And if one gets sick, it will just lie down and die. Sheep depend on people to take care of them.

Sheep are also easy prey for coyotes. I found that out early one morning.

The loud noise woke me up. The sheep were baaing and the dogs were barking. By the time I got out of my sleeping bag, Charlie was out of the wagon. He'd slipped on his boots and was holding his rifle. I jumped out the door, barefoot.

Charlie was running toward the herd. He was hollering, "HEY! HEY! HEY!"

It was just breaking daylight. I gasped at what I saw. Two coyotes had a sheep down. Wool was flying in all directions. The sheep was bellowing pitifully. It was the worst sound I had ever heard.

The other sheep began to run in all directions.

I saw Charlie raise his rifle and sight down the barrel. He pulled the trigger. One coyote took off. The other one was hidden by the sheep.

Charlie ran closer. He fired again. The other coyote ran off. They were both right out in the open. It looked like a really easy shot to me. But Charlie shot again and missed by a mile.

I ran to the sheep that had been attacked. Blood was gushing out of a big tear on its neck. It quivered and whimpered. Then it died.

I couldn't keep from crying. I'd never seen anything die before—especially in such a terrible way.

Charlie whistled and motioned for the dogs to round up the sheep. I wiped my eyes on my shirt sleeve. Charlie came close to me.

"You missed!" I accused hotly. "You didn't even hit one of them!"

"I didn't intend to," he answered.

"But they killed a sheep!" I yelled at him. I was so mad. I didn't realize I was being rude to an adult.

"If they come back, I'll have to kill them," he said softly.

"But . . . but . . ." I stammered. "You could have killed them easily. Don't you care about the poor sheep?"

"I care a lot about the sheep," he answered. "But I care about the coyotes too."

I couldn't believe what he was saying. How could he care about those vicious animals?

He handed me his rifle. He picked up the dead sheep and started walking back to the wagon. I followed, still furious with him.

He looked back at me. "You see, boy," he said. "Those coyotes don't kill sheep to be mean. They kill to live. That's what a predator does. Those coyotes are only doing what comes naturally to them."

"But sheep aren't wild animals," I argued. "And they're dumb. They don't know how to defend themselves."

"Neither does a fawn," he said. "And it's a wild animal. It's a terrible thing that animals have to die in such a way. But it's nature's way."

We got to the camp. Charlie dropped the sheep on the ground.

"I've killed a good many coyotes in my day, boy," he said. "And it's made me sick every time. But sometimes it can't be helped. I've killed a good many deer too. For food. And I don't like doing that either."

He took the gun from me and leaned it against the wagon. I looked up at Charlie. I couldn't help staring at him.

Finally I said, "I'll bury the sheep."

"No," he said. "No sense wasting it. I'll take it a mile or so away and leave it. Something will eat it. Maybe the coyotes."

He rode Kate across the meadow. He carried the dead sheep. I watched him until he was way out of sight. Then I made a fire and put the coffee on.

That night, we stayed up a little later than usual. We sat around the fire drinking coffee. I put a little canned milk in mine. It wasn't bad that way.

The sheep had bedded down. Buster and Rosie were lying near the fire.

We hadn't talked a lot the rest of that day. We just did our chores as usual. But I sure did lot of thinking. I thought about everything Charlie had said.

Charlie stirred the fire up a little with the heel of his boot.

Then he said, "Mr. Baker tells me your daddy got killed in the war. That he died saving some other fellows."

It surprised me when he said that.

"Yes, he did," I whispered.

"It's a bad thing to lose your daddy," he said. "But it's a good thing to know he died for something fine. Defending his country. And saving those fellows' lives."

I started blinking real fast. I was trying to hold the tears back. At first, I didn't want to talk about it—especially to someone like Charlie.

Then it hit me. Charlie wasn't the same person he had been when we left the ranch. Uncle Brad was right. But I still wasn't sure how I felt about him. Or how he felt about me.

I kept thinking about what he'd said. I remembered how he'd called me a young whelp and swore he wasn't going to play nursemaid to a kid who was hardly out of diapers. It still made me mad to think about it.

But suddenly, I wanted to talk about my father. And I wanted to talk to someone who had never known him. So I really opened up to Charlie.

I told him about the certificate of bravery that was hanging on the wall. And I told him about the medals. I even told him how I'd lie on my bed and hold those medals in my hands. And how I'd think of Dad dying on a battlefield so far from home.

Charlie just listened. He sipped his coffee and smoked his pipe.

I told Charlie about Dad falling out of the boat. He broke out laughing. He laughed hard and slapped his knee. And I laughed with him. It felt good to laugh again.

That night, just before I fell asleep, I heard coyotes howling. Charlie was snoring. So I figured he didn't hear them.

I listened. I wondered if they'd found the dead sheep. I hoped so. I didn't like thinking about them having to go to sleep hungry.

They howled again. And lying there in the dark, I smiled at the sound of the coyotes howling in the night.

9

Letters from Home

A few days later, Uncle Brad came into camp. He was driving his old beat-up truck.

He brought fresh supplies. He handed me a great big stew that Aunt Margie had made. And there was a freshly baked cherry pie. He also had some fresh vegetables from the garden.

Uncle Brad brought treats for everyone. He had oats for Kate. Charlie got a pouch of pipe tobacco. And there was a sack of jellybeans for me.

Boy, were we going to eat good for a while.

I liked Charlie's biscuits, potatoes, and bacon all right. I even liked the coffee now. A couple of times we'd caught fish in the stream. They were so good roasted on sticks over the open fire. And Charlie had shot rabbits and cooked them. I'd never eaten rabbit before.

But all the food that Uncle Brad brought was a real treat.

He also brought mail. There was a letter from Stan and two from Mom. Even my cousin Lois had written me a letter.

Uncle Brad said, "I'll be spending the night with you. So you can answer your mail, and I'll take it back with me."

Uncle Brad looked the sheep over. He said everything looked good.

"How's my nephew doing?" he asked Charlie.

I held my breath and waited for Charlie's answer. I didn't want to look in his direction.

It took awhile before he replied, "Oh, I guess he's earning his keep."

Earning my keep! I wanted to yell at him. You bet I was earning my keep!

I cut and hauled the wood. I helped wash the dishes and keep the wagon clean. I helped him doctor the sheep when their feet were cut from sharp rocks. And I groomed the dogs.

I peeled potatoes. I hauled water for washing dishes. And I washed my clothes when they got dirty.

I even exercised Kate a few times. And I'd never been on a mule or a horse in my life.

I would say I had more than earned my keep. That Charlie Hayes made me so mad! And I had just started to like him.

A few minutes later, Charlie got up and walked into the trees. We had made an outhouse there.

Uncle Brad waited till he was out of sight. "Earning your keep is as good a compliment as a guy can get, Jack," he said.

"Yeah, well, it wouldn't hurt him to say something nice," I said.

"He did, Jack," Uncle Brad insisted. "He did say something nice—for Charlie."

I read Stan's letter. He was making some money cutting lawns. And he earned three dollars painting Mrs. Sands' picket fence.

He added a couple of jokes at the end of the letter. Both of them were dumb. But I laughed anyway.

I walked away from camp to read Mom's letters. I sat in a grove of those trees with the light bark and the little round green leaves. Charlie had finally told me they were quaking aspens. I really liked them. The leaves rippled when a breeze went through them. It was pretty.

There was a note from Fred in one of Mom's letters.

Dear Jack,

I want you to know why I called the police. I didn't do it to be mean. You see, Jack, I knew you wouldn't have done something like that on your own. I've known you since you were born. I knew you were a good kid. But I knew if you started listening to someone, you could change. I thought it would be better if you got caught at the beginning. Before things got out of hand. I hope you understand.

Fred

I did understand. And I knew he was right.

Mom said she missed me a lot. She was working hard at the shipyard. And the victory garden was growing great.

She had ripe tomatoes and cucumbers. She'd been eating lots of spinach too. Yuck. And she'd already picked a few ears of corn. Yum.

Mom wrote a lot about Fred. I tried to read between the lines. I couldn't decide how I felt. I liked Fred. I liked him a lot.

But . . . Fred and my mom?

Dad had only been gone about a year and a half. I folded the letters up and put them in my pocket.

I wrote to Stan and Mom that night. I told Mom about the coyotes getting the sheep. I described Charlie the best I could. I discovered he was pretty hard to describe.

I liked him—and I didn't like him.

No, that wasn't true. I liked Charlie Hayes. I just didn't always understand him.

I didn't say anything in the letter about Fred. Except that I said to tell him "hi."

I couldn't believe I'd been away from home for such a long time. I was homesick. But I enjoyed being here. I liked doing what I was doing. I just wished I could tell Dad about everything. And let him know how much I liked his big brother.

Uncle Brad left very early the next morning. It was a long drive back to the ranch. And the roads were pretty bad.

For the next few days, we had a feast for every meal. Charlie's favorite was the cherry pie. He poured half a can of milk on every slab he ate.

I got over being mad at Charlie. I decided he couldn't help being the way he was. He was old and set in his ways. Besides, he wasn't so bad anymore. I was really getting to like him more every day.

Charlie *did* have rheumatism. No matter what he said. I'd seen him rubbing his legs with liniment when he was getting ready for bed. I guess he thought I couldn't see him in the dark. I didn't have to see him anyway. I could smell it.

The next month went pretty smoothly.

We'd moved the herd a couple of times. We moved to find fresh grass. There was a bigger stream by our new campsite. It was awful pretty there. I was getting to like the mountains more and more. And we saw deer almost every morning.

One morning we watched a badger digging at a ground squirrel hole. I didn't know it was a badger until Charlie told me. I never saw dirt fly so fast. Boy, could he ever dig!

Charlie said, "A badger is a very interesting animal. They say a person digging with a shovel can't keep up with a badger. And they don't care for other animals. Not even other badgers."

"Are they dangerous, Mr. Hayes?" I asked him. "To people?"

"Like most animals, they stay clear of humans if they can. But I sure wouldn't want to get one cornered."

We also saw raccoons a lot. Almost any night when we'd shine the flashlight around, we could spot one. They'd be along the creek looking for food. They'd be turning over rocks getting snails and crayfish. They were sure cute.

Charlie told me he'd had a pet raccoon when he was a boy. "You talk about an animal getting in trouble," he said. "They're a lot of fun until they get older. Then they usually get mean. And you have to turn them loose."

Late one afternoon, it suddenly turned dark. One minute the sun was shining. The next, the whole sky was nothing but black clouds.

"We're going to have a good one," Charlie said. "Let's hope the sheep will bed down before it hits."

I fed Kate a little scoop of oats. Then I tied her close to the back of the wagon. That way she'd be out of the wind a little.

Off in the distance, we saw flashes of lightning. Thunder rumbled.

We decided to eat dinner inside the wagon.

Charlie had roasted a rabbit earlier. And I opened a can of beans.

Little by little, the storm got closer. Luckily, the sheep bedded down early.

It was really dark out. They must have thought it was night. I fed Buster and Rosie under the wagon. I could tell they were both nervous.

It was a little while before the rain started. Did it ever come down! The lightning was right overhead. We could hardly hear each other talk over the sound of the thunder. It was kind of scary. But I had to admit, the lightning was dazzling against the black sky.

The dogs stayed under the wagon. But about every 15 minutes, they'd circle the herd. Charlie shined the flashlight around every time the dogs made their rounds.

Finally, Charlie said, "No use in sitting up. We may as well get some sleep."

We crawled into our sleeping bags. But I couldn't go to sleep. The storm was making me nervous.

And it was so noisy. The rain pelted the top of the wagon. The thunder cracked. And Charlie snored.

At last, the storm passed. It was about two o'clock in the morning. I finally fell asleep.

10

Bravery in the Family

In the morning, everything was soaked. Water was dripping off all the trees. The stream had risen at least a foot higher on the bank.

"It really poured, didn't it, Mr. Hayes?" I said.

"You bet it did." He handed me a gunnysack.

"You can rub Kate down. Get her as dry as you can."

Kate loved it. She kept blowing her breath on my neck. It made me laugh. Once she even nibbled on my hair.

"Hey!" I yelled. "That's not hay!"

There was some roasted rabbit left over from the day before. I fed it to Buster and Rosie. They gulped it down, nearly wagging their tails off.

The higher the sun got, the more things dried out. Charlie circled the herd with the dogs.

I made the coffee that morning. Charlie took one swallow of it. Then he spit it on the ground.

"What the devil is this?" he shouted. "Hot water?"

I thought it was just right.

Charlie dumped more coffee in the pot. Then he boiled it some more. I had to add more milk to mine.

As it got later in the morning, the lambs started getting really frisky. They were so fun. I could spend all day watching them.

They'd butt one another with their heads. Then they'd run around and around, kicking their legs high in the air.

We sat by the fire watching them. Charlie smoked his pipe. He started laughing and slapping his knee.

Two lambs were playing close to the stream bank. It was really muddy. The mud flew in the air as they kicked up their heels.

All of a sudden, one lamb slid into the water. I grabbed the crook and ran toward it. But the lamb was just out of reach.

The water was deep and swift in that spot from all the rain the night before. The lamb was bleating loudly. Its eyes were glassy with panic. It was starting to move downstream.

I knew I couldn't just stand there and watch. I waded into the stream. But it was a lot deeper than I thought.

The lamb had been pulled out into the middle of the creek by the current. I swam toward it. The current was pretty strong. But I finally got a hold of the lamb.

I was having a terrible time trying to swim back to the bank. The lamb was kicking so hard. It didn't seem to realize that I was trying to help.

Finally, I was able to stand firm near the water's edge. I tossed the lamb as high as I could. Luckily, it landed on the bank.

The lamb scrambled to its feet. It ran to its mother who was baaing wildly on the bank.

I started to pull myself out of the water. But then I heard a sound behind me. It came from the middle of the creek.

It was Charlie. I hadn't even seen him jump in. He was thrashing about in the creek. Both of his arms slapped at the water. He looked as panicked as the lamb had been.

He must have a cramp, I thought.

I swam toward him. By the time I got to him, he'd gone under. I reached down and was able to get a hold of his belt. But the minute his head got above the water, he thrashed violently. I lost my hold.

"Don't fight me!" I screamed. "Don't fight!"

Again, I got a hold of him. This time he was a dead weight. I got my arm around his neck. At last, I got him to the bank. But he wasn't moving. His eyes were closed.

Now I panicked. "Mr. Hayes!" I cried. "Mr. Hayes!"

I turned him quickly on his stomach. I straddled him and started pumping water out of him. I'd learned how in first aid class in school.

In the back of my mind, I could hear my teacher's voice. "Out with the bad air. In with the good," she had droned.

Charlie had swallowed a lot of water. After what seemed like hours, he coughed. I sighed with relief.

It took me a while to get him to the wagon. Charlie wasn't a very big man, but I had to drag him all the way. I'd turned him on his back. I put my hands under his arms and pulled him along.

Buster and Rosie came running. They were jumping all over me and barking. I guess they thought I was hurting their master.

I couldn't get him inside the wagon. He was breathing okay now. But he was weak. I brought out a blanket and put him on it. I took off his wet clothes and put dry ones on him.

After a while, he was able to sit up. He wrapped himself in the blanket. I got a fire going and heated up the coffee.

"What happened, Mr. Hayes?" I finally asked. "Did you get a cramp?"

Charlie lowered his eyes. He stammered, "I . . . I can't swim."

"What!" I exclaimed. "Why in the heck did you jump in if you couldn't swim?"

His head was still lowered. "Because . . . because I didn't know *you* could."

My breath stuck in my throat. Charlie was trying to save *me*. Even when he didn't know how to swim!

I didn't know what to say. I could have said, "You might have drowned both of us, and darn near did."

But I didn't. I was still speechless knowing that Charlie had risked his life to save mine.

I made Charlie rest that day—as long as I could.

I checked the lamb all over. He'd come through it better than Charlie and I had. I think he'd even forgotten about it.

I fixed dinner that night. I even made the biscuits. And they weren't bad. Even Charlie said so—in his way.

"Not bad," he mumbled. He didn't say much of anything else for a while.

But when we finished eating, he lit his pipe and said, "You know, boy, you saved my life."

I couldn't answer.

"I guess bravery runs in your family," he went on. "Like father, like son."

That really choked me up. I thought about Dad giving up his life to save others. Then I thought about me saving Charlie. Maybe I had inherited some of Dad's bravery.

"Mr. Hayes," I said at last. "Would you do me a favor?"

Charlie just looked at me.

"Would you please stop calling me 'boy'?"

Charlie broke out laughing. "Sure thing, Jack. And will you stop calling me 'Mr. Hayes'? It makes me sound like an old man."

We both laughed.

In bed that night, I did a lot of thinking. Mostly I thought about Dad. I knew he would have been proud of me.

I thought about what a fantastic summer it had been. And I thought about what a great guy Charlie Hayes was—when you got to really know him.

In a few weeks, I'd be going home. I was anxious to see Mom. I also wanted to see Stan and my other friends.

And I guess it's time I got to know Fred a little better, I thought as I lay there in the dark. After all, he might end up being my father.

Far off, a coyote howled. What a great sound.

I turned over and went to sleep.

About the Author

Bonnie Highsmith Taylor is a native Oregonian. She loves camping in the Oregon mountains and watching birds and other wildlife. Writing is Ms. Taylor's first love. But she also enjoys going to plays and concerts, collecting antique dolls, and listening to good music.

Other Cover-to-Cover novels by Bonnie Highsmith Taylor

For Honey
Gypsy in the Cellar
Holding the Yellow Rabbit
Indian Ghost Mystery
Kodi's Mare
Pete Ramsey and the John Thing

Summer Shepherd

By: Taylor, Bonnie Highsmith

Quiz Number: 43076

ATOS BL: 3.2   F   IL: MG

Word	GL
allowance	6
argued	4
bravery	8
crook	4
hauled	5
herd	3
mumbled	4
nibbling	3
realize	4
roasted	3